Dreams Can Come True

Stories About Hope

Book Ten

For information address Disney Press,
114 Fifth Avenue, New York, New York 10011-5690.

Printed in China
First Edition
3 5 7 9 10 8 6 4

ISBN 0-7868-3534-6

Book Ten

Dreams Can Come True

Stories About Hope

Introduction

Unconditional love helps children feel protected and allows them to believe they can do anything. Once their worlds widen, they may meet others who are smarter or more talented than they are. They may be tempted to give up their dreams, but they never should. Even when things seem at their worst, something amazing may be just around the corner.

Out of spite, Cinderella's stepsisters, in "A Magical Night," tear her pretty dress, shredding her dreams of going to the ball. But even with no dress and no hope, Cinderella discovers that her most cherished wish is granted. She goes to the ball and finds true love. In "Going Places," Dumbo has a magical dream—that he can fly. When he wakes up in the morning, he finds that this dream has literally come true!

A Magical Night

from *Cinderella*

It always seems darkest before the dawn.

Cinderella was excited. The Prince's ball was being held that night, and she was ready! She hadn't thought she'd have anything to wear. But at the last minute, her mouse and bird friends had surprised her with a beautiful pink dress that they had sewn. It wasn't as fancy as the dresses her stepsisters, Anastasia and Drizella, were wearing, but it would do.

Cinderella went downstairs to show her stepfamily. "Do you like it?" she asked, twirling for them.

Drizella recognized the beads that Cinderella was wearing. "Why, you little thief!" she cried, ripping them off. "My beads! Give them here!"

"And that's my sash!" Anastasia screeched.

Before long, they had ripped Cinderella's dress to shreds. Then they left for the ball without her.

Cinderella was heartbroken. Her dream of attending the ball was ruined. Sobbing, she raced out of the house

and into the garden. She had never felt so hopeless and alone.

"It's just no use," she mumbled through her tears. "There's nothing left to believe in."

"Nothing?" a soft voice replied. "You don't really mean that."

Cinderella looked up and gasped. A smiling old woman had appeared out of nowhere!

"Now, dry those tears," the woman said cheerfully. "You can't go to the ball looking like that!"

Cinderella could hardly believe it. The woman was her Fairy Godmother, and she was going to help Cinderella get to the ball, after all!

The Fairy Godmother looked around and spotted a pumpkin. First, she waved her wand at the pumpkin, and just like that, it was magically transformed into an elegant coach.

Next, the Fairy Godmother created gleaming white horses, a footman, and a coachman. Finally, she turned to Cinderella.

"Good heavens, child," she exclaimed as she looked at Cinderella's torn and tattered dress. "You can't go in that."

With a wave of the Fairy Godmother's wand, the torn dress was changed into the most beautiful ball gown Cinderella had ever seen! She gasped with delight.

A few minutes before, Cinderella had been sure she would never attend the ball, never wear a lovely gown, and never feel joy. Now, all her dreams were coming true!

"Oh, thank you, Fairy Godmother!" she said as she climbed into the coach. "It's more than I had ever hoped for!"

Going Places

from *Dumbo*

A good friend always believes in you.

Dumbo was the saddest and loneliest little elephant in the circus. First, his mother had been taken away and locked up. And now, the other elephants at the circus would have nothing to do with him. They looked down their trunks at Dumbo's enormous ears and decided that he was a disgrace to elephants everywhere!

One day Dumbo was lying in a pile of hay. The other elephants were ignoring him, and he was feeling very lonely.

Then a little mouse appeared and began talking to him. His name was Timothy Mouse, and he and Dumbo became friends right away. Timothy knew that Dumbo was upset about his ears.

"Ya know," Timothy said, "lots of people

with big ears are famous!" Dumbo's face brightened as Timothy continued. "All we gotta do is build an act. Make you a star—Dumbo the Great!"

Dumbo couldn't believe it. There was someone besides his mother who thought his ears were wonderful!

Even though Timothy believed in his friend, he wasn't quite sure what Dumbo would be great at doing. Then they overheard the Ringmaster talking about an idea for a new circus act: a towering pyramid of elephants. That's when the idea came to Timothy. Dumbo could jump from a springboard and land atop the elephant pyramid, waving a flag for a glorious finish!

That night, Timothy whispered the idea into the Ringmaster's ear as he slept.

Before Dumbo knew it, he and Timothy were looking on from backstage as the Ringmaster announced the act before a full audience under the big top. "I give you . . . Dumbo!" proclaimed the Ringmaster.

The elephant pyramid teetered as Dumbo ran full speed across the ring and onto the springboard. But he tripped over his ears and fell flat on his face. Then he bounced off the end of the springboard and flew out of control through the air, toppling the tower of elephants. When it was over, the elephants were bumped and bruised. The circus tent was in ruins.

After that, the Ringmaster cast Dumbo as the baby in a clown act. Dumbo was humiliated.

Then, early one morning, after Dumbo had a very vivid dream about flying elephants, he and Timothy awoke to find themselves sitting on a high branch of a tall tree. *In a tree?* How had they gotten there? Elephants couldn't climb trees! Dumbo couldn't have jumped up, could he?

Suddenly, Dumbo lost his balance. As the

two fell, Dumbo's ears caught the air and he and Timothy gently soared to the ground.

"Dumbo! You flew!" Timothy exclaimed, pointing to Dumbo's ears. "Your ears are perfect wings!" The little mouse couldn't contain his excitement. "Dumbo! The world's only flying elephant!"

It seemed impossible—ridiculous, really. And yet, Timothy never doubted his friend's ability. And because of Timothy's faith, Dumbo now had faith in himself.